THE DEVIL'S
TREASURE

THE DEVIL'S TREASURE

Sam Knight

First Print Publication January 2020

ISBN-13: 978-1-62869-034-7

ONE

NEW MEXICO TERRITORY
1851

BIG CANYON.

Sterling Chaddock stood at the rim and shook his head at the thought of the name. Who the hell could look at this and only come up with Big Canyon? It looked more like a crack in the very Earth itself than any canyon he'd ever seen.

Chaddock hadn't believed when he'd been told it was so deep that, if you were at the bottom of it, you could look up and see stars during the daytime. But the hazy cloud drifting in the enormous crevasse below him, as though he were standing on top of the highest mountain looking down, made him reconsider.

Big Canyon.

So goddamned big that birds flew around inside of it, seemingly perfectly happy to never come up to ground level. He watched a handful of vultures, too far below him to tell what kind, riding air currents and lazily chasing each other in a slow circle, looking so small they could have been flies.

Turning back the way he'd come, Chaddock put his eyes on the horizon of the mostly flat plains to regain his sense of equilibrium. Not prone to fear of heights, he nonetheless found looking down into the canyon made him feel as though he stood upon a dangerous precipice—a jagged edge between two worlds that didn't quite fit together in the right way. What was normal for his world didn't jibe with the one below.

The horse Chaddock had left tied to a stunted tree snorted and shook its head, chasing away a deerfly that had become fascinated with the horse's nose.

"Well, Mrs. Morely, what do we do now?" Chaddock asked of the big Morgan.

She blinked at him and then scratched her nose against the soft needles of the little juniper tree.

Chaddock turned and looked back out at the canyon. The bottom, hundreds, if not thousands of feet below sheer cliff walls and steep slopes, was hard to spot. "I guess I didn't think this through too well. I kind of assumed you and me would be able to just trot right on down there as happy as you please, have a look around, and trot right back up again."

He walked back to the horse, untied the reins from the tree, and stepped up into the saddle. The higher vantage point had little effect on his view.

"There has to be a way down, someplace where the whole thing gets shallow, or the crack would go all the way 'round the world, right? Split it all in half?"

Mrs. Morely didn't answer.

"Guess it don't matter." He slowly shook his head as he took in the expanse. "Even if we were down there right now, where the hell would we start looking for the treasure?"

The far side of the canyon was nearly lost in atmospheric haze, and Chaddock thought it looked like there might be even more canyon beyond it. It also looked like there might be distant clouds, maybe inside the canyon, showing the smear of rain.

Rain.

He snorted and wondered if even the ocean could fill this hole in the ground.

"Grandest sight I ever seen," he told Mrs. Morley before urging her northward. "Let's get back and tell the others we're finally here, but it might be some time before we find a way down. And maybe even longer until we find the mine."

TWO

THE SIX HORSEMEN reined their steeds at the edge of the world.

"You're right," Robert Martin said to Chaddock, "that's a goddam big canyon." Martin leaned forward onto his saddle horn with crossed arms to look out into the gaping abyss. His horse, a black mare he called Midnight, took a nervous step back from the rim as Martin's weight shifted forward.

Martin was a solid, squat man, with a long family history of mining. He claimed he was so short and broad because so many generations of his family before him had worked underground. After a few drinks, he'd wink and tell of rumors that some of his great-greats had gotten lost in the caves and eventually married women, who were of mountain cave origins, before returning to the world above.

"Ain't no way we never gettin' the wagon down there," Fred Church said, dismounting from a grey dappled mare he referred to as 'Gon'a Be Glue'. Untying his pants, he disappeared behind a bush, complaining. "Did done come all this way for nutn'."

He was a lanky, yellow-haired man with a greasy dark beard. Chaddock didn't care for him much. Church had a tendency for bellyaching, and, truth be told, Chaddock felt the man had never outgrown being a snot-nosed, mouthy kid.

"Don't seem like nutn' 'bout this 'spadition were thought out none," Church grumbled from out of sight, making sure the words were loud enough they could all hear his discontent.

Two of the other riders, brothers Warren and Timot Wells, exchanged glances with one another. They had originally come to the territories to fight in the Mexican War. When it ended, they stayed in hopes of finding gold. Like Chaddock, they didn't seem to much care for Church, but their expressions showed they were starting to agree with the man's sentiments.

The final rider, Mitchell Burke, a man with a hooked right arm and a limp on the same side, awkwardly worked his way out of the saddle and looked as though he were going to follow Church into the brush. The man was half-simpleton, as far as Chaddock was concerned, and he was nearly obsessed with Church, following the malcontent around like a chick after a hen. It wouldn't have surprised Chaddock an inch if Burke had followed Church into the brush and watched him leave a crap, which was a shame, because that was how Church treated Burke—like crap.

"Hard to see shiny stuff from all the way up here," Burke agreed with Church in his own way. "Gonna haf ta get down there somehows."

"Well you men didn't think we were just going to walk down there, pick up pockets full of silver from off the ground, and walk out, did you?" sounded a voice from behind them all.

Chaddock twisted in his saddle to see Malcom Wadsworth Lancastre, the only man he'd ever met who always introduced himself with three names, come walking up with Berthold Müller waddling along beside him.

"Actually, I seem to remember that's near exactly what you told them to expect," Müller said with a thick, meaty chuckle.

Lancastre, a tall man, walked with a stiffness, a sort of airs, that Chaddock had originally taken as disdain for anything and everything but later found out was from being shot, during a war in a land he called the Punjab. That old wound was also why Lancastre refused to ride a horse and traveled by wagon instead.

Müller on the other hand was a much rounder, red-faced man with a broom-bristle mustache that'd ruin a scythe. Chaddock didn't know who was happier there was a wagon for him to ride in—Müller himself or the horse that would have had to carry him. Chaddock thought Müller a soft man who liked being the center of attention more than nearly anything but food and drink, and he was still amazed the man was out here, so far away from the creature comforts of civilized society.

Lancastre and Müller had come from Europe together, claiming to know where the Spaniards had left a buried treasure in a barely tapped silver mine hundreds of years ago. The problem was the two foreigners had apparently been swindled by a conman almost as soon as they landed in New York, and now they didn't have the money to finance the rest of the trip.

Chaddock, Martin, Church, Burke, and the Wells brothers had all been made "partners" and promised an even split in order to convince them to join in the search. Having each bought and paid for their own provisions—as well as pitching in for Lancastre and Müller's—none of the men were much in the mood to run into problems after the two-week trip it had taken to get here.

"Perhaps I exaggerated a bit," Lancastre said, "but only a bit!" He held up one finger in an emphatic gesture. "Right, Berthold?"

"Of course!" The large man chuckled jovially. "Cursed treasure just lying on the ground waiting to be picked up by any fool who comes along and ignores the warnings!"

"I'm the fool for the job!" Burke swung a determined fist.

Lancastre, holding up a handful of leaflets, smiled and said, "This, my friends, is where Berthold and I start to pull our weight on this expedition."

Church, still behind the bush, muttered something Chaddock couldn't make out, and Burke cackled like an old woman. Martin, disgusted look on his face, pointedly turned away from the two.

"Here are copies of a map, one for each of you," Lancastre continued, ignoring the jibe and passing out the papers, "that depict part of the northern rim of the canyon somewhere near here. When we can match the terrain to this map, we will have our way down—a road the Spaniards carved down into the canyon so that they could haul silver out!"

"Didja see the size of that hole in th' ground?" Church called from his bush. "It could take years ta find what you're lookin' for!"

"Years!" Burke echoed, bobbling his head up and down.

"Not to worry!" Müller replied jovially. "All we need is to spot a rock spire formation inside the canyon the Spaniards called *Los Tres Niños*—the Three Children. There is a drawing of it on your map! Find that, and you will all be getting your deserved share of *El Tesoro del Diablo*—The Devil's Treasure!"

"Goddam, I deserve it!" Burke jumped and shouted out like a man who had just gotten religion.

"Hey, Burke! You still got that extra neck rag?" Church whispered loudly.

"I shore do." Burke stopped dancing and, patting his pockets with his good hand, pulled out a kerchief.

"Jesus Christ, Burke," Chaddock said. "Don't give it to him!"

Church guffawed from behind his bush. "How 'bout a copy of that map, then?"

THREE

THE FIRE ILLUMINATED the canyon wall above the camped expedition, putting Chaddock on edge as he lay on his bedroll. He hadn't expected the little fire to have such a large effect. Up top, a campfire was easy to bank and hide from distant eyes, but here, on a wide ledge halfway down into the canyon, any light that escaped flickered across the towering rock walls, lighting them up a hundred feet into the night and casting shadows bigger than biblical giants. From a distance, Chaddock thought, it would be noticeable as a lighthouse beacon, but he worried that instead of warning unwary ships away, it would be summoning the bold and the curious, and maybe the depraved, from miles around.

So that he didn't have to see it, he rolled over and settled himself looking out over the cliff and into the night. Although the Havasupai, the people Chaddock had been told lived in the area, were purportedly friendly, Chaddock had no experience with them and didn't want to find out the hard way.

He found himself staring up at the dark silhouettes of 'Los Tres Niños' against the starry night sky. The unique configuration of three spires had not been hard to find. Müller had spotted them from miles off, almost as easy as if he'd already known where they were. Chaddock had to admit they did kind of look like three children, each wrapped in a blanket held closely over their shoulders and all huddled closely together for protection. It was easy to imagine them frozen in time, standing in a circle and looking down sadly at something only they could see.

"Tell me 'gain whys't we can't see the rest of that map?" Church's voice echoed out into the canyon with no regard for how much noise he made or who might be listening. Lancastre's response was more properly muffled, but Chaddock didn't need to hear it anyway. He knew it by heart now. Church hadn't given up on the question since first seeing the partial map they'd used to find the top of the road, two days ago.

Lancastre and Müller were convinced that the only fair way to find the treasure was if everyone found it together, and they were sure, now that the expedition had found the ancient road down into the canyon, that they would all walk straight to the mine tomorrow. Of course, they had thought everyone would make it down to the bottom of the canyon in less than a day, too.

If they had all been on horseback, or better, on mules, that might have happened, Chaddock reckoned, but bringing the wagon down the "road" had proven impossible. The wagon, six oxen, and all six horses had been left above with Müller, who, upon seeing the vague trail that was most definitely not a road, had quickly volunteered to stay with them. The rest of the expedition had continued down on foot, carrying packs of mining equipment and food supplies on their backs, following the narrow, loose graveled, crumbling, five hundred-year-old path that had obviously never been intended for anything more than a single person at a time when it was at its very best.

Which it certainly was not now. Centuries of erosion had completely erased it in some places and turned it into piles of rocks in others.

Chaddock's legs still ached from the constant downhill walk of the day, not to mention the parts where they'd used finger and toeholds to cross cliff faces. He had no idea how any of them where going to climb back up, let alone carry untold riches worth of silver out.

When this relatively large, flat spot had presented itself in the late afternoon, the men unanimously decided to make camp rather than continuing on and risking spending the night trying to sleep on a ledge or falling off in the dark. They'd all slipped more than enough times to be wary.

"Mebbe I'll just take it from you." Church's voice again, echoing out into the still night of the canyon.

"Maybe you ought to bed down for the night." Martin's voice rose up nearly as loud as Church's had been, but carried a heavier threat. "Been a long day, and tomorrow's like to be longer yet."

Another muffled comment from Lancastre, followed by the sound of quick movement, coaxed Chaddock into rolling over to see what was going on. Church, his cheeks ruddy from more than the glow of the campfire, was trying to stare down Martin, Warren, and Timot while Burke nervously looked on, not sure what to do. For a moment, Chaddock thought Church might go for his gun, but the man cursed and turned his back on the rest of them, choosing instead to stalk his way to his bedroll and drop onto it.

Somewhere, far below, a coyote howled. Chaddock rolled back over and looked out again. He fell asleep wondering what the Tres Niños were looking at that made them so sad.

FOUR

THE FULL SUN BEAT down upon the men as they continued down the trail, its steep, narrow slope ensuring there was no shade to be had next to the cliff. The greenery below called invitingly to the men, even occasionally sending up whiffs of fresh smells, but they had all become weak-legged and stumbly after two nearly days of walking downhill, and the tops of the trees were still a hundred feet or more below them if they'd been going straight down rather than angling slowly in.

"Anyone got any water left?" Church called out.

"I do," Burke, limping ahead of Chaddock, said. He twisted his head sideways, and using his good hand, pulled his waterskin strap from around his neck and out from under his bum arm. He handed the waterskin back to Chaddock who handed it to Warren to pass to Church.

"Obliged!" Church said when the skin reached him. He tilted his head back and emptied the last of the contents into his open mouth, letting it fill and overflow into his dark beard. He used his free hand to rub the spilled water into his whiskers and around his face with a loud, self-satisfied "Ahhhh!"

The empty waterskin flew past Chaddock's head, startling him, and landed on the ground in front of Burke. The half-lame man stumbled as he tried to come to a stop and pick it up. His pack overbalanced him and tipped him forward, threatening to pull him off the trail and over the cliff. Burke's break in rhythm threw off Chaddock's stride and, in turn, Warren's, bringing them both to a stumbling halt and eliciting a loud curse from Church as he had to stop walking as well.

"Stupid bastard," Warren muttered as Burke, visibly shaken, regained his footing.

"Yeah! Come on, Burke!" Church hollered.

"Wasn't talking about that one," Warren said.

Reaching level ground was a godsend, and Chaddock found his knees couldn't hardly handle walking normal anymore. Here, the bottom of the canyon was wide enough to host a copse of trees and, after the narrow path, it felt nearly like being out on the wide-open plains.

"Goddam! Goddam!" Burke looked like he wanted to dance a jig, but his bad leg wouldn't leave the ground as he hopped around. "Din't think we's ever gonna hit bottom!"

Lancastre, who hadn't complained once while walking stiffly down the cliff trail for the last two days, dropped his pack and carefully sat on a chair-sized rock, wiping sweat from his face with an already soaked handkerchief. "I suggest we all take a short break and consider setting up a basecamp right here at the bottom of the road."

"Road, he says," Church said to Timot. "Tha' were a road same a whore's a good God-fearin' woman!"

Timot ignored the comment. "Sounds like flowing water over that way," he said to the rest of the group, pointing toward the thickest greenery. "I'm going to go see if I can find some to lie down in for a spell. I'll meet the rest of you back here."

"I'll come with you," Warren said. "I could use a swim, even if it's inna teacup."

"I think we should all stay together until we find the treasure!" Lancastre's voice raised in pitch as well as volume.

"Don't worry about them," Chaddock said. "Where are they gonna go? Where are any of us going to go?" He turned and pointed at the path they'd just come down. "That's the only way out that we know of, and it would take at least two days to get to the top, probably longer as I suspect going up will be worse than coming down. Maybe even longer, if we're carrying any more weight than we already are. I don't think you need to worry about any of us running off with more'n our share of anything."

Lancastre glanced back up the trail and then at the exhausted men around him. "You are right, of course." He pulled his waterskin off his belt. "Mr. Wells?" he called after the brothers, not seeming to care which one responded. "Would you be so kind as to consider filling this for me if you happen to find your bed of water?"

FIVE

THE FIRE AT THE NEWLY established basecamp had already burned low and dinner was near ready by the time the Wells brothers returned, both looking clean and refreshed.

"I take it you boys had a good time?" Chaddock asked. He'd already made several trips down to the water to refill waterskins and fill the cookpot and coffee pot. The two brothers had found a near perfect swimming hole that had also provided a nearly three-foot long fish with an odd humpback Chaddock was fixing up for dinner.

"Almost worth the walk down." Timot looked sideways at Chaddock. "Almost."

"Passable," Warren said with a grin.

"Oh good, you've returned!" Lancastre stood, holding a book. "It's well time I showed this to everyone then." He opened the book and pulled out an ancient folded parchment from between the protective pages. "I only wish Berthold could be down here with us. This was his dream, after all."

"Fat pig couldn'ta rolled down here if he was pushed." Church elbowed Burke in the side.

"Nope! Nope. Couldn'ta." Burke shook his head and grinned.

Lancastre gave them a withering look, but the two men were unfazed.

"El Tesoro del Diablo," Lancastre said, unfolding the delicate map and trying to hold it so everyone could see. "The Devil's Treasure."

They all stood and came closer to make out the scrawls on the yellowed parchment.

As they examined the map, Lancastre spoke on. "According to legend, the mine was abandoned to the devil, the already mined and smelted silver left behind and considered cursed."

Chaddock shrugged and went back to the cookfire. The map, while definitely a map, held no magical secret beyond a poor sketch of details and directions on where to go next.

"Bah! Müller already told us all that. Ain't no devil gonna keep me away from the good stuff!" Burke spat, stepping even closer to look at the map.

"The legend says thirteen men lost their souls to the devil—who came in person to collect them," Lancastre continued. "The mine was abandoned, against orders, and the surviving men, all holding true to their story, chose to be put to death for treason rather than return to work the mine."

"Give it a rest," Burke said. "The haint stories didn't scare us away when Müller told them, they ain't gonna work now!"

"Not after takin' damn near three weeks ta get here, anyways," Church added.

"Stories are made up to keep thieves away," Martin said. "Every mine is cursed unless you still want workers digging in it. Every miner says his mine is haunted unless he wants some fool scoutin' it."

"I still ain't see what was so secret as you couldn'ta showed us the map afore now!" Church disgustedly turned away from the aged parchment and pointedly stalked off. For once, Burke, still craning his neck to stare at the map, didn't follow him.

Warren pointed to the line representing the road they'd taken down into the canyon. "If this is anything to scale, we still got a ways to go before we get to the mine. That's what, two, mebbe three side-legs of the canyon over?" He ran his finger along what appeared to be dead-end canyons the trail went past. "Hell, this looks like it goes farther along the canyon bottom than the road down was long."

"Shhhheeeeeeet," Church cursed from where he was digging in his pack. "I ain't surprised. This trip's like pickin' taga-longs offa wool blanket—it just don't never end, and it's leavin' me ragged!''

SIX

"I DO WISH BERTHOLD were here to see this!" Lancastre dropped the map to his side as he gaped at the dark hole in the canyon wall. Framed by two giant cottonwoods, the mine entrance, which had been shaped from a jagged crack at the top and widened by hand at the bottom, was nearly hidden behind a mess of catclaw brush, and loomed half-again taller than a man. "He wanted this so badly. It's all he's talked about since the day I met him."

"Yeah, yeah. Heard all that afore," Church said, looking at the mine. "Where's the treasure?"

"Yeah! Where's all the shiny stuff?" Burke spoke in a way that reminded Chaddock of a grunting hog. "I ain't see no silver nowheres!" He limped toward the mine entrance, kicking at the dirt as though he should be exposing nuggets. "You and Müller said it was just waitin' here, layin' on the ground, ready to be picked up by any idiot what finds it, but I don't see it!"

Whether Lancastre heard or was lost in thought, he didn't respond. He folded up the map, gently secured it in between the pages of the book, and then stowed it away in his pack as the rest of the party slowly began to follow Burke toward the mine.

"Goddam stinks over here!" Burke complained, coming to stop and waving his good hand in front of his nose. He kicked at the ground some more and peered into the brush.

"Hold up!" Martin called.

"Find somethin'?" Burke lit up and turned to see.

"Look at those rocks over there." The squat man pointed to an overhang in the cliffside with three large boulders under it. "See the markings carved in the rock? It's a warning of death."

Carved into the stone were ancient markings, Indian scratchings, Chaddock had heard them called. He'd been told, by a saddlebag preacher, that they were false stories of the past and graven idols of heathen gods. That same preacher had later gotten drunk and spent the contents of the collection plate in the local brothel.

Warren and Timot stopped following Burke and dropped their packs to the ground, looking exasperatedly from the mine entrance to Martin. Following Lancastre's map hadn't been any easier than finding the road down into the canyon, or walking it, had been, and it had taken another day to get to this point.

"Aww, bullshit!" Burke flapped his bad hand at it dismissively. "It's some Indian pup's finger draw of a goddam turtle! I'm a get me my silver!"

Church guffawed and exaggeratedly slapped a raised knee. "You tell 'em, Burke!"

"Perhaps we should listen to Mr. Martin," Lancastre said, but Burke was already nearing the mine entrance.

"Burke! Stop!" Martin called. "It's a booby trap! The real mine is that a way." He pointed past the carvings, back around the bend they'd just come from.

"Go get tha' shiny stuff, Burke!" Church called, not following the man. "We're all right behind ya!"

"Burke!" Chaddock called. "Hold up!"

Burke ignored him and kept walking.

"Goddam stinks—" Burke was interrupted by the scream of a mountain lion. The sandstone colored beast, nearly as large as Burke, leapt out from the bushes and shouldered Burke aside, spinning the man around as it raced past him. Caught surrounded by men, the big cat zig-zagged in confusion, skidding to a halt and looking around wild-eyed. With another scream, it shot past Lancastre and vanished off into another arm of the canyon before anyone had been able to get a shot off.

"Hell of a booby trap!" Church laughing, holstered his pistol. "How'd they keep that thing in there all those years?"

"That wasn't the trap," Martin grumbled.

Burke, on the ground, rolled to his side and struggled to right himself using his good arm and leg. "Yup. Tha's why it stinks over here. Smells like goddam cat piss inna sun!"

SEVEN

CHADDOCK AND THE OTHERS looked over Martin's shoulder as he pointed to the carvings in the rocks.

"These are Spaniard's marks," he said.

"As they should be!" Lancastre agreed. "But what do they mean?"

"This heart, with the crack through it, warns that anyone searching for treasure here will find misery."

"Yeah, yeah. Broke heart. Cursed mine," Church said. "So what?"

"Yeah, so what? I found misery already," Burke said. "I smell like goddam cat piss now."

"You did afore!" Church grunted.

"So," Martin answered Burke, "it means they set up a booby trap. A lot of miners do that to protect their mines when they are away. Look here." Martin pointed to the drawing that looked like a turtle. "See how his tail points that way? That means the real treasure is over that way. The obvious mine shaft we see may have been where they dug out the silver, but not where the treasure is. It's a decoy or a trap to keep people away from the treasure."

"What's the four squares on the turtle's back mean?" Warren asked, pointing to odd markings inside the squares that divided up the turtle shell.

Martin shook his head. "Maybe how far away to look? Maybe how much treasure is in there. I don't know the symbols. They are probably from the local people."

"What's this?" Timot asked, calling attention to the backside of the adjacent boulder that had nearly hidden the turtle carving on the cliff. Everyone shuffled around and peered to see another image, one that couldn't be seen unless you stood between the boulder and the cliff wall. It looked like a strange man with giant, pointed teeth, claws, and a tail. Low on the giant boulder, the drawing was hidden just out of sight of casual observation. Unlike the other carvings, it was highlighted with white paint.

"Never seen one like that," Martin said. "Maybe it's to scare off the locals? Might be a warning of the curse. It's probably supposed to be the devil." Martin stared at it a moment longer. "Or it might be pointing back to the mine with those claws…"

"Pointing at it?" Burke huffed. "Lookit here." Nervously, he indicated faded scratchings around the image that hadn't been painted white. It looked distinctly like the crooked top of the mine entrance. "That's the devil comin' *out* a the mine!"

"Buncha hogswaller," Church cursed. "I say we go look *in* the mine!"

Chaddock, curious, walked around the third boulder to see if there were any more markings. Near the bottom, on the cliffward side, hidden where he wouldn't have seen it if he hadn't been searching, was etched a small, rounded cross.

"Here's something else," he told Martin.

Martin moved to have look. Burke pushed in alongside, craning his neck to see.

"Ha!" Burke cried out. "X marks the spot! Buried treasures for sure!"

"No…" Martin ran his fingers across the bottom of the cross and rubbed off caked dirt from past flood waters. Hash marks appeared under the cross. "This is a grave marker. For thirteen people."

EIGHT

THE CAMPFIRE BLAZED bright, lighting the canyon wall for what felt like miles to Chaddock. He would have rather not had a fire at all than have one damn near big as a bonfire, but he'd been outvoted. He sat with his back to the fire, so he could keep watch and see if anyone approached their sheltered offshoot of the canyon. He was tired of listening to all of the bickering anyway.

The rest of the men still squabbled about the dangers of going into the mine, looking for where treasure was actually buried, not finding silver lying on the ground, the lack of supplies because it had taken days longer to get here than expected, and anything else they could think of at this point.

Church, and of course Burke, wanted to go into the mine proper, and they were upset they'd been talked out of going back when it had still been daylight out. Martin had reached the point he was all for letting them go and had actively started encouraging it, daylight or not. Timot, usually the quieter of the two brothers, was pushing hard to follow the turtle's tail as an indicator of where to go look for the treasure. Warren was backing him up, and Lancastre was trying his best to mediate it all.

"What about you, Chaddock?"

The question startled Chaddock out of his reverie. The arguing voices had all blurred together and started to lull him. He looked back over his shoulder to find they'd all gone quiet and were looking at him expectantly.

"What?"

"We need a tie-breaker," Lancastre said. "Mr. Church, Mr. Burke, and myself believe we should explore the mine first thing in the morning. Mr. Martin and the Misters Wells would like to search the other way, where they believe the markings indicate the treasure is hidden. That leaves you as a deciding vote, Mr. Chaddock."

Chaddock looked at all the eyes, glinting in the firelight, waiting for his reply. The anxiousness on their faces worried him, and he was surprised Lancastre had managed to mediate even a momentary truce.

"Let me think on it. I'll let you know in the morning," Chaddock said.

"Goddam it!" Church took of his hat and threw it on the ground. "Figures!"

"Goddam it!" Burke echoed, nodding like a broke-neck mule.

None of the others said anything, but the sighs of exasperation were audible over the crackling fire.

NINE

RUMBLING EARTH WOKE CHADDOCK. Though the fire was down to nothing but coals, the dim glow still allowed him to see all of the others sitting up as well. Almost all of them. Two of the bedrolls were empty.

The smell of dust suddenly filled the camp.

"God help them," Martin said, looking at Burke and Church's empty bedrolls. He shook his head and laid back down.

"We should go after them!" Lancastre began getting up.

"You want to risk your life digging out loose and falling rock in the dark?" Martin asked. "I'm not going near that mine until I've given it a good thrice-over in full daylight and made sure there isn't another trap. It's not like I didn't warn them."

The Wells brothers glanced at each other and laid back down as well.

Lancastre looked to Chaddock.

"He's not wrong," Chaddock said.

When Lancastre finally laid back down, Chaddock did as well.

TEN

THE PALE, THIN DAWN, made even weaker at the canyon bottom where the sun wouldn't hit for hours, found the remaining expedition members standing in front of the mine entrance, squinting in the dim light to make out the extent of the damage.

"I don't think they could have survived," Warren said, looking at the pile of rubble coming out of the opening. It appeared as though a landslide had come out from farther inside the tunnel, filling it with boulders and dirt.

"Depends on the trap," Martin said. "This could have been set to shut them in and close up the entrance, not kill them."

"Why would anyone bother with such a trap?" Lancastre asked. He looked tired and much older than when Chaddock had first met him. "One that doesn't kill, I mean."

"If you set a false trigger near the rockslide, which, like any pile of rocks is hard to disguise," Martin answered, "and someone thinks they got past it, they may not notice if the actual trigger is farther in. They would die either way, of course, but the hidden trap is more likely to be successful."

"Or maybe it was a trap to keep something in if it tried to come out," Timot said.

"You let that fool Burke get into your head, didn't you?" Warren chastised his brother. "There ain't no devil in that mine nor any other'n."

As if in answer, a deep rumbling growl shuddered out of the mine, followed by the faint sound of calling voices.

"I'd say they survived," Chaddock said.

ELEVEN

FOLLOWING MARTIN'S EXPERT ADVICE, the five men had made good progress removing rubble by midday. As the heat of the sun finally reached the canyon bottom and began to beat down upon them, they began to slow in spite of Church and Burke's begging calls. They all had bloody hands and sore backs from digging and moving rocks ranging from gravel to the size of a man.

"Ought to just let the fools lie in the grave they made for themselves," Martin mumbled to himself.

Chaddock had overheard Martin mutter several such comments, but they had all been personal grumbles, nothing actually intended to talk the others out of digging. Chaddock was sure everyone had similar thoughts though, and, as the day grew hotter, the complaints became louder and more frequent, but none of the men stopped digging. Not even Lancastre, who, with his bad back, had to lift each of the rocks from a deep-knee bend without leaning over to pick them up.

Another deep rumble came from somewhere deep within the mine, shaking the ground under their feet. They all froze and warily watched the rocks around them, ready to run at the first sign of another slide. Burke and Church screamed for help again, picking up enthusiasm that had waned over hours. It had become near routine.

"Shut up already, we're coming fast as we can," Martin muttered for the umpteenth time. "It's just rocks settling and the earth talking."

A large rock broke free and rolled down from the top of the pile, startling them all and sending them scrambling out of the way. The sounds of Burke and Church's calls grew suddenly louder and Chaddock looked up to see the place where the boulder had been now exposed a dark opening through to the inside of the mine.

Church's pale face appeared in it.

"Jesus Christ Almighty! Get us the hell out of here!" he cried. His greasy black beard had turned gray with dust.

"Out! Out! Out!" Burke's voice floated up as he shouted like a scared child.

"Workin' on it!" Chaddock answered, picking up the rock that had rolled down and tossing it aside. "Hold your horses!"

"We're coming for you," Lancastre assured them.

"Somethin's in here!" Church screamed. "Hurry up! I can hear it coming!"

Another deep rumble came from within the mine again, but this time, without the rockslide muffling it, it sounded more like a roar.

"Out! Out! Out!" Burke barked, his face pushed in next to Church's, filling in the hole as they both desperately pushed at the rocks in their way, trying to make the hole bigger. "Out! Out! Out!"

Church put a hand on Burke's face and shoved him back while sticking his own head through the growing hole.

"Get back, you idiots!" Martin shouted. "You'll trigger another slide and bury yourselves!"

There was another earth-shaking rumble, and a ruddy light appeared behind the two squabbling men, backlighting them. They stopped fighting long enough to turn and look, eyes widening and faces slackening with horror.

Burke screamed with a primal fear that came out as nothing more than a prolonged grunt. Church's was shrill and short.

"What the hell...?" Warren dropped the rock he'd been carrying and stared up at the strange light streaming out of the mine. His brother did the same.

This time, there was no doubt the sound they heard was a roar. One that put the mountain lion's to shame.

Church turned back to the opening and scrabbled at the rocks like a madman, trying to force his body through the still-too-small hole. Chaddock, quickly followed by Warren and Timot, scrambled up to the top of the rubble pile to reach Church. The man had his head and one arm through, grasping desperately for Chaddock's hand. Chaddock caught his hand and pulled.

Church grunted as his body pressed against the rocks, but he shouted, "Pull harder!"

Chaddock adjusted his footing and his grip on Church's hand, then Church was suddenly yanked backward and disappeared.

His scream echoed out of the mine, and was suddenly cut short.

Chaddock, thrown off balance from losing Church's grip, slipped and fell. Warren and Timot caught him and helped him get his feet back under him.

"What happened?" Timot asked.

"I don't know. It was like he got pulled outta my hand."

Chaddock scrambled back up and reached the hole just ahead of the brothers. Inside, light filled the tunnel, revealing a stunned, slack-jawed Burke, sitting at the top of the other side of the pile of rubble and staring down at Church's bodiless head.

Its mouth worked silently, brushing the beard on its chin back and forth, mixing the muddy pool of blood it lay in.

Burke's mouth opened and closed just as silently.

"Jesus Christ," Warren whispered as he peered in next to Chaddock.

"What is it?" Timot asked from behind them. "What happened?"

Chaddock reached an arm in and slapped the dumb-struck Burke on the shoulder. "Burke!" he hissed. "Come on! We've got to get you out!"

Burke slowly turned his head toward the hole, but his eyes remained glued to Church's. The dead man's mouth slowly stopped moving and the life faded out of his eyes.

"Out?" Burke whispered.

"Yeah, out. Come on!" Chaddock grabbed a handful of shirt and started pulling the man.

"Out! Out! Out!" Burke suddenly cried and lunged for the hole, knocking Chaddock and Warren back into Timot. "Out! Out! Out!" Burke clawed and pushed at the rocks, triggering a slide of rubble that took the other three men down to the bottom in rough fashion, half burying them, and Lancastre, in the process.

A monstrous roar thundered out from within the mine again, shaking the ground as much as the landslide had.

"Out! Out! Out!" Burke screamed, still grabbing and pulling at the rocks around the opening. "Out! Out! Out!"

And then he was gone.

The light from the tunnel seemed to flicker, and then everything went silent but for the panting of the four terrified men outside of the mine.

TWELVE

IT LOOKS LIKE THEY used that giant boulder and those timbers to block that side passage, probably to shut that thing in." Martin drew in the dirt next to the campfire as he spoke. "When Burke and Church set off the trap, the shaking must have loosened the supports. And then, whatever that thing was, it must have pounded against the boulder until it finally got through."

Chaddock nodded in agreement. That fit with what he'd seen as they'd taken turns peeking into the mine. With the setting sun, the light inside the mine had changed, leading them to believe it was sunlight, coming from the newly exposed passage, that lit the mine, not the flames of hell as they had all been first quite ready to believe.

Lancastre sat next to the fire with his head hung low. It was the first time Chaddock had seen him sit anyhow but ramrod straight. None of them had any doubts as to whether Burke was still alive. He'd left a curled-up arm lying next to Church's head.

There had been a lot of discussion about leaving, about abandoning the mine back to the devil that they no longer had any doubt was real, but the side passage that let the light in had exposed something else they'd all seen as well: the walls were spiderwebbed with silver veins.

"I still think we should follow the turtle's tail and look for whatever treasure was left *outside* the mine," Warren said.

Timot shook his head, as did Martin.

"If that *is* sunlight," Martin said, "then that thing, that devil, or whatever it is, is already outside of the mine somewhere. Who knows how long it will take to find a way around to where we are now?"

"If it could get over here, then why would they have bothered to shut it up in there?" Warren argued. "I think were safe on this side of that rockslide."

"I'm not willing to take that chance," Timot said, siding against his brother for the first time Chaddock had seen. "You saw what happened to Burke and Church. And how fast it happened. I say we leave. Before it happens to us."

"I agree. I think we should leave," Martin said. "What good is finding a treasure if you end up dead?"

Chaddock nodded, feeling much the same, and looked to Lancastre, who hadn't said anything for at least an hour now.

Slowly Lancastre began to nod his head. "You are right, of course, Mr. Martin. The stories were obviously true. The devil has claimed two more souls. If that was sunlight we saw in the cavern, it could feasibly find a way around to where we are. And if that wasn't sunlight, if it was something from the pits of hell, then my guess is any treasure we find actually would be cursed. Dare we risk our own lives, perhaps even our very souls in pursuit of material wealth?"

He pursed his lips and looked at the faces of the men around the campfire.

"It is hard to give up a dream, especially when we are this close, and Berthold will be so disappointed. But..." He shook his head. "I can bear no more guilt upon my soul. In the end, those men are dead because I brought them here. I cannot be responsible for any more. And I am sure Berthold will feel the same way. No matter how badly he wanted this, he couldn't have known what would happen. He couldn't have known the legend of the curse was real.

"My God, he loved telling that story." Lancastre rubbed his face tiredly and sighed. "We should leave at first light."

THIRTEEN

EVERYONE WAS PACKED before first light, but fog, rolling in from the river had settled over the canyon floor, making an oppressive gloom they could hardly see through. Chaddock kicked dirt over the last of the coals and buried the fire as soon as they could see the ground well enough to walk. Looking up at the patches of gray sky that appeared and disappeared through the fog layer, Chaddock thought about how he'd been told you could see the stars during the day from the bottom of Big Canyon. It wasn't true, the sky, what you could see of it, was just as blue as it was up top, but the nights were a lot longer and darker down here.

"I have something I want to do before we go," Lancastre said. With a small pickaxe in hand, he went over to the boulders with the markings on them and kneeled down next to the one with the cross carved into it. It was hard for Chaddock to see what Lancastre was doing in the dim light and foggy haze so thick it drifted between them in waves, but the scratching sound was enough for everyone to realize he was adding two more marks to the thirteen already there.

"All right," Lancastre said, standing up stiffly, using the boulder for support. "I'm ready."

The men looked at each other for a minute, all feeling as though something should be said. The night before, they had discussed trying to retrieve the head and the arm and burying them, giving Burke and Church some kind of proper send off, but in the end, the risk had seemed too great and they had just stopped talking about it.

The sound of a falling rock interrupted the silence.

They all turned toward the mine entrance, still not visible in the cliff face that was nearly black against the pale sky.

Another rock fell, this one accompanied by loud snuffling sounds.

"We need to get out of here," Timot whispered.

The men silently, but expeditiously, gathered up their packs and headed in the direction of the road, trying not to trip on rocks and shrubs suddenly appearing out of the meandering fog. They hadn't gone more than a hundred yards when they heard more rocks falling and then a rolling rumble, like another small landslide.

Then they heard the roar. Even muffled in the fog, it echoed through the canyon, and deep within their souls.

"It's out." Timot's voice shook.

"Keep moving," Warren whispered hoarsely.

The men picked up their pace to a trot. The tin cup on Chaddock's pack came loose and began clinking against the handle of his pickaxe, ringing like a bell out into the pre-dawn fog with every step he took. Still hurrying, he spun the pack off his back and tore the cup off, snapping the leather strap that held it on, but it was already too late. The roar sounded again, closer this time, despite the distance they had covered.

"Jesus, it's fast!" Martin gasped as he drew his pistol.

Chaddock threw the tin cup as hard as he could, hoping it would make a sound that led the beast away from the men. The cup arced through the air and disappeared into the fog, clanking once before going silent, as if landing in sand.

Almost immediately Chaddock heard impossibly heavy footfalls and then the rustle of brush in the direction he'd thrown the cup.

"Christ!" Timot's voice squeaked as the not-so-distant sound of movement through bushes suddenly turned into the sound of limbs cracking off of trees.

"Shut up!" Warren hissed at him.

Timot stumbled as he drew his sidearm.

Lancaster's stiff gait hindered him, making him fall behind, and Chaddock slowed for him. Lancastre, face pinched, shook his head and silently waved him on insistently.

The thumping drew closer to the jogging men, and Chaddock could feel the vibrations in the earth under him. Timot panicked, breaking into a sprint, not trying to be silent anymore. "Oh, God!"

Warren huffed a curse and sped after his brother as they disappeared into the fog ahead of them. Martin quickly changed his direction, breaking away from where Timot and Warren had gone, heading toward the canyon wall, and then he vanished into the mist as well. Chaddock glanced back to see Lancastre still struggling to keep up.

Three shots rang out, the source hidden in the gray world ahead of them.

Someone, probably Timot, Chaddock thought, screamed. The scream cut short, ending so abruptly it was almost as if it had never happened at all.

Four more shots sounded.

Chaddock stopped and turned back for Lancastre, catching him by the arm and pulling him at a right angle from the direction they had been running and opposite the way Martin had gone.

"What are you doing?" Lancastre huffed breathlessly.

"We can't outrun it," Chaddock whispered best as he could, "the bastard is already ahead of us. And Martin just went down a dead end."

"Where do we go?" There was fear in the man's eyes, but he held it firmly under control.

"The river," Chaddock told him. "We head for the river. It's our only chance."

Two more shots and another scream and Chaddock thought both brothers were gone.

"If it's an animal, it should be content with its kills," Chaddock said. "We just have to find a way to quietly get past it without reminding it we're here."

"That's no bloody animal!" Lancastre shook as he spoke. "It's the devil himself, come for our souls!"

"Maybe. If so, I'll face him on my terms, not his," Chaddock said, drawing his own pistol.

FOURTEEN

THE SUN WAS HIGH, and the fog gone. Chaddock and Lancastre had heard one more shot, much farther in the distance, and assumed it was Martin. Then they had reached the river and the sound of the flowing water prevented them from hearing anything else—assuming there was something else to hear.

Lancastre struggled to keep up but didn't complain. Chaddock felt going slow and quiet was safest anyway.

Sometimes walking along sandbars and other times climbing over boulders, they followed the river upwards until it looked as though it would veer away from the northern cliff face with the road.

"I think I can see the road, there," Lancastre said, pointing ahead to the distant cliff as they rested.

Chaddock could make out a vague diagonal line coming down and nodded agreement. "We should aim for where it looks to touch bottom. Do you think you can make it that far before sundown?"

"I'll bloody well die trying!"

"I hope not."

Walking a steady pace, the two men did their best to stick to the cover of the sparse tree lines of the canyon bottom. They'd heard no more roars, no gunshots, no screams. By the time they reached the road, sunset was upon them and exhaustion had long settled in. Quietly encouraging each other, they moved forward on sheer willpower alone.

"I've never seen such a glorious sight," Lancastre puffed. The top of the canyon wall glowed copper as the low sunlight bathed it in the last of its light against a velvet purple sky.

Lancastre walked so stiffly now Chaddock could hardly believe the man was still on his feet, but he went straight to the head of the road.

"Are you up for that?" Chaddock asked. "In the dark?"

"I don't know how far I can go," Lancastre admitted, "but I want as high as I can get before I collapse. I want out of this God-forsaken place."

Chaddock nodded. He felt the same way. They had both been starting at the slightest sound ever since leaving the rushing roar of the river, constantly looking over their shoulders, and pushing on. Chaddock kept finding he'd drawn his pistol without realizing it and then putting it away when his fingers cramped from carrying it.

"You go first." Lancastre waved him on. "I don't want to slow you down. I'll be right behind you, as soon as I catch my breath."

Much as Chaddock had feared, climbing up was harder than coming down had been and, exhausted as he was, Chaddock managed no more than fifty steps before he feared his legs would give out and he had to stop. Leaning against the cliff wall, he looked out into the canyon, even now still awed by the sheer size of it all. Big Canyon, he thought, shaking his head as he looked out over the treetops and toward the whitewater river raging through the bottom.

That's when he spotted it, walking hunched over and sniffing along the ground, following their trail like a dog. The beast was the size of a tree and walked like a man, and it looked like nothing Chaddock had ever seen.

It had an oversized head with dagger-like teeth he could see from here, arms ending with sickle claws, a tail thick as a tree trunk—and it was colored the bright red of the deepest embers in a firepit.

It had to be a demon.

Chaddock looked down. Lancastre hadn't even started up the road yet.

"Psst!" He tried to get Lancastre's attention. "Psst!"

Lancastre finally glanced up, and Chaddock waved for him to hurry and pointed toward the approaching demon. Lancastre's eyes widened, and he started up the slope with his pained, stiff walk. He only made it a dozen or so steps before he slipped, sending loose gravel sliding.

The demon's head popped up at the sound, and Chaddock felt it lock eyes on him even from this distance.

It roared and began running toward them.

"Hurry!" Chaddock yelled to Lancastre, drawing his gun. "It's coming!"

Lancastre tried to pick up his pace but in doing so slipped again, falling down this time. The demon's thumping footfalls grew audible as it closed the distance quickly.

"Hurry!" Chaddock called again.

Lancastre made it another four steps before falling again.

Chaddock took steps toward him, slipping and sliding down the loose rock of the trail.

"Go, damn you!" Lancastre yelled as he struggled to his feet. "Get higher! Get away!"

Then the demon was there upon them, its enormous head just as high as Lancastre up on the cliff. Chaddock emptied his pistol at the creature, but it never slowed as it leaped across the final few yards and snapped Lancastre off the ledge with one bite of its massive jaws.

Chaddock watched in horror as the demon threw back its head and, with two more snaps of it jaws, swallowed the man down its gullet.

Fumbling at his pack for more powder cartridges and lead balls, Chaddock fought to reload his pistol with shaky hands. The demon roared at him, and leaped up, snapping it teeth together with a sound like the greatest of axes chopping wood, but Chaddock was barely out of its reach.

It tried climbing the road as Chaddock reloaded, but its wide body couldn't balance on the ledge hardly wider than one of its feet, and it slipped off several times before giving up and, roaring in rage, started clawing and jumping at the canyon wall below Chaddock.

Chaddock shoved down on the ramrod lever of his pistol, pressing the lead balls tightly into place against the powder already in the cylinders. One by one, methodically, he repeated the process until all six cylinders were loaded. Then he emptied his gun into the demon's head again. It roared and hissed at him. Blood spots appeared on its hide, the dark red looking nearly black on its thick, flame colored skin, but the bullets had no effect.

As the sun went down and the light faded, Chaddock reloaded his gun again.

And again.

FIFTEEN

MR. CHADDOCK! WHAT A SURPRISE!"

Chaddock looked up, startled to see Berthold Müller standing at the top of the canyon rim. The oversized man was holding a chunk of roasted meat in his fist and smiling jovially with grease running down his chin. The sight surprised Chaddock. He had been walking up the difficult trail, one step at a time, one foot in front of the other, for so long now, that he'd stopped paying attention to how far he'd come or how far was left to go.

Müller's ruddy cheeks and bristle mustache seemed strange and otherworldly, something completely out of place in Chaddock's personal reality of plodding steps, heat, loose rocks, and exhaustion.

"The others didn't make it," Chaddock croaked. He'd run out of water the day before.

Müller held out a fleshy hand and pulled him up the last step. "Of course they didn't." He took another bite of the meat in his free hand before tossing it over his shoulder, laughing. "They never do!"

"They never—?" The scene before Chaddock finally registered to his eyes as he tried to make sense of Müller's words. Of the six oxen and six horses left in Müller's care, only one ox and two of the horses remained, all tied to the wagon. The others were all bloody, rotting carcasses, scattered around the camp, torn apart as though by packs of wolves and now surrounded by swarms of flies.

"What have you done?" he finally managed to ask.

Laughing, Müller, still holding Chaddock's hand, pulled Chaddock in close to him. "I warned you," he said. "I warned all of you. Many times over. It is a cursed mine. A cursed treasure." The soft fleshy hand turned hard in Chaddock's grip. "The Devil's Treasure," Müller said, cocking his head. "*My* treasure."

He grinned, and his mouth stretched impossibly wide, revealing unnatural, jagged rows of sharp teeth. "Mine all mine…" He laughed at his own joke.

Chaddock tried to pull away from him but couldn't.

"You didn't think I would actually let anyone have *my* treasure, did you?"

"You led us here on purpose." Chaddock fought to get his hand back, but Müller's grip was unbreakable.

"Of course. It's been over three hundred years since my baby ate a real meal, and I grew weary of waiting for someone to find her. No matter how many maps I passed around, no one seemed to make it all the way out here, and she was getting soooo hungry. It was way past time to let her come out and play again. You were just the greedy idiots for the job."

"You're a bastard."

"I'm the original bastard." Müller let go of Chaddock and, at the same time, shoved him hard, throwing Chaddock backward toward the cliff.

Chaddock desperately grabbed at Müller as he fell, barely catching hold of his sleeve. The fabric ripped and gave way, but it was enough to prevent Chaddock from going over the edge. He scrambled away from the ledge, circling around Müller, who laughed all the while.

Chaddock drew his pistol.

"Go ahead!" Müller grinned wider, showing all his horrible teeth, and stuck out his chest. "Bullets can't hurt me."

The pistol shook in his hand as Chaddock kept it trained on the thing that had called itself Müller.

"What's wrong, Chaddock? No stomach for killing another man?" Müller laughed and shook his head. "Oh well."

A tongue, black as night and long as a whip, shot out of Müller's impossibly wide mouth and wrapped around

Chaddock's wrist, yanking him forward to land sprawling in the dirt at Müller's feet.

"Now," Müller said, bending down and easily lifting Chaddock up by the front of his shirt, "why don't you go on back down there and feed my little girl?"

"I don't think your 'little girl' is hungry anymore," Chaddock snarled, struggling in Müller's grasp like a helpless child.

Müller began walking toward the edge, holding Chaddock high enough his feet couldn't touch the ground. "She's always hungry."

Chaddock realizing he would never be able to break the impossible grip, reached behind his back to his waistband and pulled out a long, dagger-like tooth with blood still caked on it.

"Not anymore," Chaddock said, holding it up between his and Müller's faces.

Müller's eyes widened.

"She's all full of lead now. I fed her all I had."

Plunging the tooth deep into Müller's fleshy chest, Chaddock spat in the face of the thing that was not a man.

Stunned, Müller dropped Chaddock and looked down at the protruding makeshift weapon. His wicked grin faded into an angry snarl. "You—"

Chaddock kicked him off the cliff.

Müller's roar of rage stopped short when his falling body hit an outcropping, but the fall continued, his bulbous body rolling and bouncing down the cliff until Chaddock couldn't make it out anymore.

"Church was wrong. You could make it with a little push."

Chaddock fell to his knees and stared out into the abyss.

Big Canyon, he thought. Goddamned big canyon.

The sound of a nickering horse broke the silence. Shakily, Chaddock stood and turned to look at the big Morgan tied to the wagon.

"Well, Mrs. Morely, what do we do now?"

ABOUT THE AUTHOR

A Colorado native, Sam Knight spent ten years in California's wine country before returning to the Rockies. When asked if he misses California, he gets a wistful look in his eyes and replies that he misses the green mountains in the winter, but he is glad to be back home.

As well as having been Distribution Manager for WordFire Press and Senior Editor for Villainous Press, he is the author of five children's books, four short story collections, three novels, and nearly four dozen short stories, including two media tie-ins co-authored with Kevin J. Anderson, one for Planet of the Apes and one for Wayward Pines.

A stay-at-home father, Sam attempts to be a full-time writer, but there are only so many hours left in a day after kids. Once upon a time, he was known to quote books the way some people quote movies, but now he claims having a family has made him forgetful, as a survival adaptation.

He can be found at SamKnight.com and contacted at Sam@samknight.com.